Twinkle, twinkle, little star,
How I wonder what you are!
Up above the world…

…so high.

Many of the rhymes can be acted out as you share them. This can be an important way for children to remember them.

Poor Jack's falling on his head.

Oh dear!

Spend time talking with children about the pictures. This increases their pleasure in the book and gives them a chance to make sense of the rhymes.

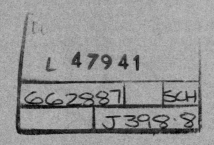
First published 2001 by Walker Books Ltd
87 Vauxhall Walk, London SE11 5HJ

2 4 6 8 10 9 7 5 3 1

Original selection © 1996 Iona Opie
Illustrations © 1996 Rosemary Wells
Introductory and concluding notes © 2001 CLPE/LB Southwark

This book has been typeset in Monotype Bembo

Printed in Hong Kong

British Library Cataloguing in Publication Data:
a catalogue record for this book is
available from the British Library

ISBN 0-7445-6867-6

MY VERY FIRST MOTHER GOOSE

edited by
IONA OPIE

illustrated by
ROSEMARY WELLS

WALKER BOOKS
AND SUBSIDIARIES
LONDON · BOSTON · SYDNEY

Jack and Jill went up the hill,
To fetch a pail of water;
Jack fell down and broke his crown,
And Jill came tumbling after.

Mary, Mary, quite contrary,
How does your garden grow?
With silver bells and cockleshells,
And pretty maids all in a row.

Hey diddle, diddle,

the cat and the fiddle,

The cow jumped over the moon;

The little dog laughed

to see such fun,

And the dish ran away

with the spoon.

Humpty Dumpty sat on a wall,

Humpty Dumpty had a great fall.

All the king's horses and all the king's men

Couldn't put Humpty together again.

Sing a song of sixpence,
A pocket full of rye;
Four and twenty blackbirds
Baked in a pie.
When the pie was opened,
The birds began to sing;
Wasn't that a dainty dish
To set before the king?

Here we go round
the mulberry bush,
The mulberry bush,
the mulberry bush;
Here we go round
the mulberry bush,
On a cold and
frosty morning.

Little Jack Horner sat in a corner,
Eating his Christmas pie;
He put in his thumb, and pulled out a plum,
And said, What a good boy am I!

Down at the station, early in the morning,

See the little puffer-billies all in a row;

See the engine-driver pull his little lever –

Puff puff, peep peep, off we go!

Diddle, diddle, dumpling,

my son John,

Went to bed with his trousers on;

One shoe off,

and one shoe on,

Diddle, diddle, dumpling,

my son John.

Baa, baa, black sheep,
have you any wool?
Yes, sir, yes, sir, three bags full.
One for the master,
and one for the dame,
And one for the little boy
who lives down the lane.

Pussy-cat, pussy-cat, where have you been?
I've been to London to look at the queen.

Pussy-cat, pussy-cat, what did you there?
I frightened a little mouse under her chair.

Bobby Shaftoe's gone to sea,
Silver buckles at his knee;
He'll come back and marry me,
Bonny Bobby Shaftoe.

To market, to market, to buy a fat pig,
Home again, home again, jiggety-jig.

To market, to market, to buy a fat hog,
Home again, home again, jiggety-jog.

There was a crooked man,

And he walked a crooked mile,

He found a crooked sixpence

Against a crooked stile.

He bought a crooked cat,

Which caught a crooked mouse,

And they all lived together

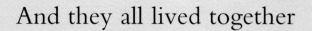

In a little crooked house.

I had a little nut tree, nothing would it bear
But a silver nutmeg and a golden pear.

The king of Spain's daughter came to visit me,
And all for the sake of my little nut tree.
I skipped over water, I danced over sea,
And all the birds in the air couldn't catch me.

The big ship
sails on
the alley
alley oh,
The alley
alley oh,
the alley
alley oh;
The big ship
sails on
the alley
alley oh,
On the last
day of
September.

Little Boy Blue, come blow your horn,

The sheep's
  in the meadow,
The cow's
  in the corn.

Where is the boy
  who looks after the sheep?
He's under a haycock
  fast asleep.

Will you wake him?
  No, not I,
For if I do,
  he's sure to cry.

Pat-a-cake, pat-a-cake, baker's man,

Bake me a cake as fast as you can;

Pat it and prick it, and mark it with **T**,

Put it in the oven for Tommy and me.

Wee Willie Winkie
runs
through
the town,
Upstairs and
downstairs
in his

night-gown,
Rapping at the window,
crying through the lock,
Are the children all in bed,
for now it's eight o'clock?

Twinkle, twinkle, little star,
How I wonder what you are!
Up above the world so high,
Like a diamond in the sky.

Read it again

Pat-a-cake

You can make cakes out of modelling clay to the rhyme of "Pat-a-cake". Children can add letters from their names and from family and friends' names.

Here's B for Bobby.

And here's D for Daddy.

Wall poster

Children can choose one of their favourite rhymes to illustrate by drawing or painting a picture. You can add the rhyme in large writing to make a wall poster. You can read it together regularly and get to know it really well.

That's a great sheep.

He's all curly.

Tape it

When your child has heard the book read many times, they will know some of the rhymes by heart. You can make a tape of them singing familiar rhymes to play and enjoy with the book.

Ready? Here we go.

Diddle, diddle, dumpling, my son John...

Mary, Mary, quite contrary,
How does your garden grow?

With silver bells and cockleshells,
And pretty maids all in a row.

Act the rhyme

The rhymes "Baa, Baa, Black Sheep", "Mary, Mary, Quite Contrary", "Pussy-cat, Pussy-cat" and "Little Boy Blue" are written as if two people were speaking. You could begin, leaving space for your child to join in as the other person.

Rhyme time

Get together any toys that could help children to act out the rhymes in this book: trains, a bucket, toy animals, a dish and spoon, for example.

Humpty Dumpty
sat on a wall…

Humpty Dumpty
had a great fall.

Other versions

There are many different versions of Mother Goose nursery rhymes. These include collections from different countries and cultures, like the Caribbean for example. Share this rich variety with your children and talk together about rhymes that are the same or different.

Reading Together

Red Books 2-4 years

Yellow Books 3-5 years

Blue Books 4-6 years

Green Books 5-7 years